# Zachary Z. Packrat
## and His Amazing Collections

BASED ON A TRUE STORY

by Brooke Bessesen

Illustrations by Jenny Campbell

# A prelude about
# PACKRATS AND THEIR MARVELOUS MIDDENS . . .

THE TERM "PACKRAT" STARTED AS A NICKNAME for many wood rat species (scientifically called *Neotoma* spp.) that make their homes in North and Central America. These small, soft-eyed rodents live in nearly all terrains—alpine tundra, forests and woodlands, grasslands, chaparral, desert scrub, and tropical thornscrub.

A packrat's nest (home) is concealed by a midden, an archaeological term meaning "garbage pile." Packrats gather items to pack into their middens from up to 300 feet away. They love to collect small, shiny objects, as well as twigs, leaves, pollen, bones, reptile scales, human artifacts, shells, insect parts, and a favorite—scat (animal poo). Some packrats on the run will drop one item for another, earning their other nickname, "trade rats."

Packrats urinate (pee) on their middens to mark the territory as theirs. Because packrats don't drink much water, their urine is viscous (thick) and dries into a crystallized, amber resin called "amberat," which cements all the items together into a solid mass. Generations of packrats can create enormous middens several feet wide and thick.

Researchers find some of the best-preserved middens in caves and under rock overhangs in the desert regions of the American Southwest. Since the 1960s, paleoecologists (scientists who study prehistoric ecosystems) have discovered middens dating back to the late Pleistocene epoch (Ice Age). Using 14C (radiocarbon) dating, some middens have proven to be at least 40,000 years old! And because mummified remains of plants and animals are perfectly preserved, these middens provide clues about the surroundings of that time. For example, one packrat midden in Utah revealed a bone from a giant camel that's now extinct. And another near Las Vegas — currently a desert with few trees — shows evidence that a coniferous (pine) forest once grew there. Wow!

So while the "junk" in a packrat's midden may seem worthless, it can offer valuable information for us to study. People who store a lot of stuff also are called "packrats." Some collect things such as antique furniture, sports memorabilia, or autographs, while others keep crumpled tinfoil, stacks of shoe boxes, or piles of magazines. They save what makes them happy or what they believe will become valuable. One way we learn about people who lived before us is by studying their belongings. Archaeologists dig for ancient human possessions. Museums safeguard treasures of art and history. We even know details about our own families through heirlooms our ancestors passed down.

Yes, packrats are important — both animals and humans! By collecting and preserving items, we can better understand our past and how the world has changed through the years.

I know a real packrat named
ZACHARY Z.
who has enough stuff (I'm sure you'll agree).

He lives in a bungalow
FILLED to the brim
with thousands of knickknacks that barely fit in.

He never puts ANYTHING into the trash!
Instead, he will stash it somewhere in his cache.
He likes to save things he might use down the line:
a single BRASS BOLT or a twist of OLD TWINE.

Collections are always displayed with great pride,
and glass-covered hutches clutch RICHES inside,
like fragments of eggshell in various hues,
and good seed reviews clipped from *Packrat Towne News*.
Ten shiny gum wrappers,
six oddly shaped poos,
some bundles of lint,
and a roadrunner's shoes.

For artwork, Zach has the keen eye of a pro
and owns SEVERAL PAINTINGS by Gopher van Gogh.
He also has sketches of scrumptious pommes frites,
and oodles of doodles drawn by Beetle's feet.

KETCHUP

HOW does he do it? And WHY, you might ask?
To keep so much stuff well preserved is a task.

You see, for a packrat it has to be done.
It's part of his NATURE, it's how he has fun!

But like every packrat, Zach has to have more!
MORE things for the walls . . .
and the shelves . . .
and the floor.

So off he skedaddles, knapsack on his back,
and searches for GOODIES to put in his pack.
Although room is scarce, not an inch here or there,
he brings home new tidbits and stows them with care.

One day he recovered a tattered WOOL SOCK he found on the ground out by Sniffing Nose Rock.

That sock keeps him cozy on cold winter nights.

It's SWIFT as a sled.

It stores small delights.

And when the winds rise that sock FLIES to great heights!

Monday through Sunday, Zach keeps to his quest,
but Saturday mornings are always the best,
since that's when one packrat can TRADE with the rest!

Fossilized Poos $1.00

Browsing the bargains along Swap Meet Street,
he greets other packrats and hunts for a treat.
Some things grab his interest with such great allure,
his challenge is choosing **WHICH things** to procure.

Maybe SEVERAL of those.

Who knows when he might need doll clothes for his toes?

No matter how silly an object might seem,
Zach feels it is worthy to hold in esteem.
If questioned at all, he'll reply with a groan,
"A treasure's not measured by money alone!"

His favorite belonging, the thing held most dear,
can always make Zachary grin ear-to-ear.
This packrat's prized piece? An antique so unique . . .
One BAMBOO KAZOO with a "perfect pitch" squeak
passed down through the years as a family heirloom
with great-great-great-Grandpapa's QUAIL COSTUME,
a pinch of EAR WAX, a real ARROWHEAD,
a FULL SET OF JACKS, and some petrified bread.

FORMAL QUAIL COSTUME WITH FULL PLUMMAGE

Zach thinks that these links to his past play a part
in keeping his ancestors near to his heart.
Plus, he LOVES old things for the clues they bestow —
a peek at how packrats once lived, long ago.

When thunderstorms threaten
and Zach stays indoors,
he dusts his belongings
and finishes chores.

Then off he skedaddles, KNAPSACK on his back,
through damp twisting tunnels
and one narrow crack,

to visit a place that is truly adored . . .
The Midden Museum, where history is stored.

Inside, he investigates each of the halls
and peers at rare RELICS that line the long walls:

ancient PINECONES from an ancient pine tree
and tiny white SHELLS
from when desert was sea.

A RING from a king
with a stone from his throne,

A SABER-TOOTH'S TOOTH

and a *giant* SLOTH'S BONE.

With all this grand stuff and the insight it brings,
Zach gets so excited—he
ZIPS and he ZINGS—
that once the sun shines,
he starts searching for . . . THINGS!

MORE things for the walls
and the shelves
and the floor.
Like every good packrat,
Zach has to have MORE!

I'll bet you have met a real packrat or two.

If so, then you'll know what I've said is all true.

They cherish MEMENTOS from family and friends,

TRINKETS and TREASURES, and strange ODDS and ENDS.

It might seem like rubbish, but let me daresay,

that clutter of JUNK may gain value someday.

Besides, it is packrats like Zachary Z.
for whom such possessions create utter glee!

Knapsack on his back, Zach is happy to roam
and rummage for DOODADS to put in his home.

His bliss is a bungalow filled to the brim
with thousands of KNICKKNACKS
that barely fit in.

# Questions for Discussion

Do real packrats play a valuable role in the environment? Why?

Why are some people called "packrats"?

Do human packrats play an important role in preserving history?

Why are items from the past important? What can we learn from them?

Do you collect anything? Why do those items have value to you?

Based on those items, what would someone in the future know about you?

What are antiques? What are heirlooms?

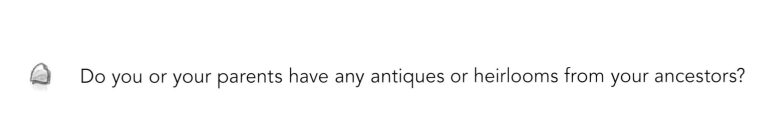 Do you or your parents have any antiques or heirlooms from your ancestors?

What do antiques and heirlooms tell us about our own families?

Are museums important? Why?

What can we learn from ancient or buried civilizations?

Do you know a packrat? Who is it? What does he or she like to collect?

Are you a packrat?

Designer MARY WINKELMAN VELGOS
Photography PAUL AND JOYCE BERQUIST
Color Separation AMERICAN COLOR

Text BROOKE BESSESEN
Illustrations JENNY CAMPBELL

FOR YOUNG IMAGINATIONS and ARIZONA HIGHWAYS are trademarks
of the Arizona Department of Transportation, parent of *Arizona Highways*.

Published by the Book Division of *Arizona Highways*® magazine,
a monthly publication of the Arizona Department of Transportation,
2039 West Lewis Avenue, Phoenix, Arizona 85009.
Telephone: (602) 712-2200

Website: www.arizonahighways.com

Publisher: Win Holden
Editor: Robert Stieve
Senior Editor/Books: Randy Summerlin
Creative Director: Barbara Glynn Denney
Production Director: Michael Bianchi
Production Coordinator: Annette Phares

Production Date 8-1-10
Plant & Location Printed by Everbest in Guangdong, China
Job/Batch# 95599

ISBN 978-1-932082-83-8
Library of Congress Cataloging-in-Publication Data
Bessesen, Brooke.
Zachary Z. Packrat and his amazing collections: based on a true story / written by Brooke Bessesen;
illustrated by Jenny Campbell.
    p. cm.
Summary: Rhyming text introduces a packrat who spends his time finding interesting objects to bring home,
where he uses them to decorate, saves them to trade at the swap meet, or simply stores them for future use.
Includes facts about packrats and discussion questions.
[1. Wood rats—Fiction. 2. Collectors and collecting—Fiction. 3. Stories in rhyme.] I. Campbell, Jenny, ill. II. Title.

PZ8.3.B4637Zac 2008
[E]—dc22
                    2007012589

For Mom and Dad, two beloved packrats—
thank you for saving so many family treasures
and showing me the importance of preserving
the past.
   bb